Jem Digs Up Trouble

GOLDTOWN BEGINNINGS

★ ★ ★ 4 ★ ★ ★

Jem Digs Up Trouble

Susan K. Marlow

Illustrated by Okan Bülbül

KREGEL
PUBLICATIONS

Jem Digs Up Trouble
© 2020 by Susan K. Marlow

Illustrations © 2020 by Okan Bülbül

Published by Kregel Publications, a division of Kregel Inc.,
2450 Oak Industrial Dr. NE, Grand Rapids, MI 49505.

ISBN 978-0-8254-4628-3, print
ISBN 978-0-8254-7628-0, epub

Printed in the United States of America
21 22 23 24 25 26 27 28 29 / 5 4 3 2

Contents

New Words

ain't—a poor way of saying "am not," "are not," or "is not"

bedroll—a rolled-up blanket

burlap—a rough fabric used for sacks

canteen—a metal container that holds water, with a strap for carrying

flannel—soft fabric made of wool or cotton

grub—food

kinfolk—family

long johns—underwear with long legs and long sleeves

pay dirt—ground that contains enough gold to make it worth mining

pesky—annoying

suspenders—straps that hang over a person's shoulders and hold up their pants

varmint—a pest

CHAPTER 1

A Muddy Creek

Swish, swish, swish. Sand and water swirled in Jem's gold pan.

Rattle, rattle. Gravel and small rocks banged against the sides.

The morning sun beat down on Jem's head.

His hat kept the sun out of his eyes, but it could not keep out the heat.

Jem felt like it had sucked him dry.

The August heat had almost sucked Cripple Creek dry, too. It was only a muddy trickle.

A muddy creek was not good for washing gold. It was hard to see flakes or nuggets in brown water.

"You're mighty dirty, young'un."

Jem looked up. Strike-it-rich Sam squatted a few feet away.

Mud dotted the old prospector's wrinkly face and his beard.

Strike's pants and red-flannel shirt were also caked with mud. So were his suspenders.

Jem grinned. "You're muddy too."

Just then Nugget joined Jem. The golden dog pushed his nose close and whined.

Pet me! he seemed to say.

Jem put down his gold pan and ruffled Nugget's golden fur. "Where have you been?"

Nugget shook himself. Dust flew up in a big cloud.

"Pesky dog!" Strike waved his hands and coughed. "Rolling in the dirt again."

Jem sneezed. *Ah-choo!* His eyes watered.

Then he hugged Nugget. "He's not pesky. Have you seen any rattlesnakes this summer?"

Strike grunted and scooped creek dirt into his pan.

"Nugget is the reason you haven't," Jem said. "He keeps tarantulas and gophers and other varmints away."

When Strike didn't answer, Jem filled his gold pan. He would wash gold one more time this morning.

Then I'm going to play with Nugget.

"It's hotter than blazes around here," Strike muttered.

The old miner was right about that.

Sweat dripped down Jem's face and neck. It trickled down his back and arms.

Only his hands and bare feet felt cool. Brown creek water dribbled over his toes.

"It's time for me to get away from this heat," Strike said. He dumped out his pan. "I'm thinkin' of goin' off on a prospecting trip."

Jem's heart leaped. "Up in the mountains?"

Cool breezes. Icy-cold creeks. Sparkling water.

"Yep." Strike pointed to the tall mountain peaks. "I've heard about some gold strikes up there."

"What kind of strikes?" Jem asked.

Strike chuckled. "Rich ones."

Jem's heart thumped even faster.

Strike-it-rich Sam was always going off on prospecting trips. Like four months ago, when he found Nugget.

Strike had never struck it rich. Not yet, anyway. But bringing home a hungry golden dog was better than finding gold.

At least Jem thought so.

"Yes sirree," Strike was saying. "There's gold up there. I can feel it in my bones."

Jem's ears pricked up. "How long will you be gone?"

"Oh, two weeks or so," Strike said. "It takes time to find just the right spot."

"That's for sure." Jem looked at the muddy brown trickle. "This is not the right spot."

Strike laughed. "You got that right. I'm gonna strike it rich up there someday."

Jem's thoughts buzzed louder than a swarm of bees. Maybe Strike really would hit pay dirt this time.

And maybe . . .

"I wish I could go with you." Jem's words came out fast.

Strike's bushy eyebrows went up, like he was surprised. "You want to come along?"

Jem nodded.

Strike slapped his knee. "That's a jim-dandy idea, young'un. It gets mighty lonesome on the trail."

Jem's mouth fell open. "Really?" Strike wanted his company?

"We're partners, ain't we?"

"We sure are!"

How could Jem forget? Whenever Pa was too busy to pan for gold, Jem took his place alongside Strike.

Like today.

"I'm almost eight years old," Jem said. "I could be a real help on the trail."

"You could at that, I reckon." Strike smiled.

Jem beamed. "When do we leave?"

"Hold your horses, young'un." The miner pointed to a big canvas tent and a black cookstove not far uphill from the creek. "Take a look."

Jem followed Strike's pointing finger.

Pa was walking into camp. He held a shotgun in one hand. A wild turkey hung over his shoulder.

Jem's mouth watered. *Yum!* "Turkey for supper!"

It had been many weeks since the Coulter family enjoyed such a fine feast.

"That ain't what I meant," Strike said. "It's not me you got to ask. It's your pa."

Jem's cheerful thoughts went *pop!*

Would Pa and Mama let him go prospecting in the wilderness with Strike?

Jem slumped. Probably not. At least Mama probably wouldn't.

Mama worried enough when the family went blueberry picking up in the hills each fall.

She worried about bobcats, mountain lions, and bears.

She especially worried about grizzly bears.

Mama would not want to worry about Jem for two weeks.

Strike pulled himself up from the rocky creek bed. "Well, partner. What are you waiting for? Let's go ask your folks."

CHAPTER 2

Birthday Surprise

Jem leaped to his feet. "Yes, sir!"

Strike was a grown-up. Pa and Mama might say yes if he asked them.

Jem grabbed his gold pan. He dumped out the rocks and water. Then he followed Strike up the dry, crumbling bank of the creek.

Dust puffed up with each step.

"Come on, Nugget!" he hollered.

Barking, Nugget jumped up.

Jem could run fast, even with bare feet. He and Nugget raced past Strike. They ran all the way to the Coulter family's tent.

It wasn't far.

"Pa!" Jem shouted. "Mama!"

Jem's little sister Ellie pushed open the tent flap and stepped outside.

"What happened?" she asked. Her eyes sparkled with excitement. "Did you hit color?"

Jem stopped short. "Just because I hollered doesn't mean I found gold."

Ellie let out a big breath. "Why else would anybody around here yell like that?"

Jem rolled his eyes. *Silly little sister.*

Pa laughed. "She's got you there, son." He dropped the turkey on a nearby tree stump. "I thought the same thing."

"If you didn't wash a big gold nugget, then why *are* you shouting?" Mama asked.

Strike walked up just then. "Mornin', folks," he said cheerfully.

"Strike's going on a prospecting trip in the mountains," Jem said. "He wants me to go with him. Can I go? Please?"

Please, God, let Mama say yes.

Mama didn't say yes. She didn't say no.

She said something else. "*May* I go."

Jem bit his lip. Mama was always fussing about the way he and Ellie talked.

She had more to say. "I declare, Jeremiah.

17

You and Ellie have run wild all summer long." She crossed her arms over her chest.

Mama was right about that. It had been Jem's best summer ever!

Mama was still not done talking. "It's a good thing school starts up in a few weeks."

Jem groaned, but just to himself. He didn't want to think about school. Not ever.

"*May* I go with Strike?" he asked again.

Pa looked at their friend. "Are you really going off on another prospecting trip?"

"Yep." Strike waved his arm toward Cripple Creek. "I can't wash nothin' from that muddy trickle."

Pa sighed. "I know. The rocker has stood empty since the end of July."

Jem peeked around Pa. Their rocker box sat on the creek bank. Jem could throw a rock and hit it if he wanted.

Gravel, water, and dirt had rattled down that funny-looking contraption all spring.

Pa and Strike had found gold with it. Not much, but enough to keep working their claims.

But a rocker box needed water to do a

good job. A *lot* of water. More than a gold pan needed.

Pa would have to wait for the winter rains to use the rocker again.

"May I please—"

Pa held up his hand. Jem stopped talking.

Strike laughed. "I did invite the young'un to go along." He winked at Pa. "I hear he's got a birthday comin' up pretty soon."

"I do!" Jem agreed.

Strike chuckled. "Eight years old."

Jem nodded and stood on his tiptoes. He had to look older . . . and bigger.

Pa's dark eyes twinkled. "That's so."

"A prospecting trip would be just the thing for a boy's eighth birthday," Strike said. "It gets mighty lonesome on the trail with only a donkey to talk to."

Tingles raced up and down Jem's arms. Strike was a good talker. He could explain what a good idea this trip was. Jem was sure of it.

"We could keep each other company," Strike added.

"Hmm," Pa said. He looked at Mama.

Mama's forehead was scrunched up in

worry wrinkles. "I'm not sure I want Jem going so far away from home."

Jem held his breath and didn't say a word.

Instead, he talked quietly to God. *Help Strike say the right words.*

Mama looked at Pa. Then she looked at Strike. More worry wrinkles appeared.

"Aw, Ellen." Strike laughed. "You know the young'un is safer with me than in his own tent."

The wrinkles in Mama's forehead went away. She uncrossed her arms. They hung down by her sides.

She smiled. "You're right about that, Strike."

Jem let out the breath he was holding. *So far, so good.*

A minute went by. Then another. It looked like Mama was thinking hard.

"He may go," she said at last, "so long as it's all right with Matt."

"It's fine with me," Pa said. "He'll have a jim-dandy time."

He smiled at Jem. "You might even hit pay dirt. We could trade in this tent for a real house."

A thrill went through Jem. "You can count on—"

"Yippee!" Ellie whooped.

Jem spun around.

Ellie was clapping and squealing.

She grabbed Strike's mud-speckled hands and did a little dance. "Hurrah, hurrah!"

"Roasted rattlesnakes, Ellie!" Jem hollered. "What are you so fired up about?"

Ellie stopped dancing. She stopped squealing. She let go of Strike's hands.

She looked at Jem with wide, happy eyes. "We get to go prospecting with Strike."

We?

Thud! Jem's heart dropped to his stomach like a big, hard rock.

CHAPTER 3
Packing Up

Jem stared at Ellie. He felt sick inside.

Strike said this was an eighth-birthday prospecting trip. Ellie wasn't eight years old. She wasn't even seven.

Ellie had turned six just one week ago.

No fair! Jem swallowed his hot words.

Even if he wanted to shout his words, he didn't get a chance. Ellie was talking.

His little sister talked all the time. She could chatter faster than a scolding squirrel.

"When do we leave, Strike?" Ellie began to hop and dance again. Her dark-red pigtails slapped her shoulders.

"Today? Tomorrow?" she asked. "What should I pack? Can we bring Nugget?"

Jem sucked in a big breath. "Roasted rattle—"

"Jem." Pa cut off Jem's favorite saying with firm words. "Be still."

Jem snapped his mouth shut.

"Let's go for a walk, Ellianna," Pa said. He held out his hand.

"Sure, Pa!" Ellie grabbed Pa's hand and skipped along beside him.

They headed for Cripple Creek.

As soon as Pa and Ellie left, Mama smiled at Jem. "Your sister is too little to be gone overnight in the wilderness. Pa will explain it to her."

Jem's whole body slumped in relief. Hurrah for Pa and Mama!

"Go pack your warm clothes, your long johns, and some extra socks," she told him.

Jem wrinkled his forehead. "Long johns?"

Whoever heard of wearing scratchy long underwear in August? *Ugh!*

"It's cold in the mountains at night," Mama said. "Even during the summer."

She looked at Strike. "Anything else?"

"Aw shucks, Ellen." Strike's shoulders went up and down. "He don't need much."

He winked at Jem. "We prospectors travel light. It saves room for all the gold we'll bring home."

Jem laughed.

"Canary will pack our gear into the hills," Strike said. "Gold pans, shovels, picks, grub, a frying pan, bedrolls—"

Hee-haw! Strike's scruffy gray donkey laid his ears back and gave the miner a mean look. *Hee-haw!*

"You see?" Strike poked a thumb over his shoulder. "He's raring to go."

Jem shook his head. Canary did not look raring to go anywhere.

The donkey looked like he didn't want to carry a heavy pack on his back. He looked like he wanted to stay home and eat grass.

Even if the grass was dried up and dead.

"Go on, Jem," Mama said. "Get your things together."

Jem took off for the big tent where his family lived.

"We're leaving at first light, young'un," Strike called. "Bright and early. We got a long way to go."

"I'll be ready!" Jem yelled back.

He ducked under the tent flap and stood up.

Air as hot as an oven hit him. Jem could hardly breathe.

He stepped around a small potbelly stove in the middle of the tent. A stovepipe went up and out a hole in the canvas ceiling.

Jem didn't like that stove. It took up too much space. He was always bumping into it or stubbing his toes.

Pa never lit the stove. But he would not take it out, either. "Some cold winter day, you'll be glad it's here."

So far, Jem was *not* glad. Winters were not very cold in California.

Plus, stoves inside canvas tents were scary. The half-burnt tents in Goldtown told Jem it was better to keep a woodstove far away from a tent.

"I'm glad our big cookstove is outside," Jem said, yanking the wool blanket from his cot.

He rolled it up and stuffed it in a burlap sack.

Jem pulled his socks, a red-flannel shirt, and his long johns out of a wooden crate.

Sweat trickled down his forehead. "Just because I pack my long johns doesn't mean I have to wear them."

He made a face. "It's too hot."

Into the burlap sack they went, but only because Mama said they must.

He found his boots under his cot and dragged them out.

"Jem?"

Jem spun around.

Ellie stood next to the tent flap.

Her face was red. Her eyes were watery. She sniffed.

Jem wiped the sweat from his face and sat down on his cot. "What?"

"Have a good trip." Ellie gave him a tiny smile. "Bring home lots of gold."

His sister looked like she was trying hard not to cry.

Suddenly, Jem's heart hurt. *Poor Ellie!*

Hardly any children lived on the gold claims along Cripple Creek. Only a few more lived in Goldtown.

Ellie was a good playmate. She and Jem did everything together.

They delivered pies on Saturday afternoons.

They caught bullfrogs to sell to the café.

They panned gold side by side.

They chased wild turkeys and caught baby bunnies.

They explored coyote holes together.

No wonder Ellie thought she would be going along on this prospecting trip!

Jem got up from the cot. "I'm sorry you can't come."

He meant it.

"Me too." Ellie rubbed her eyes.

Before he could change his mind, Jem hugged her. "Maybe when you turn eight, you can go with Strike on a prospecting trip."

Ellie's face lit up. "You and me and Strike, right?"

Jem smiled. "Yep. All three of us."

"Yippee!" Ellie's tears stopped.

Just like that.

CHAPTER 4

On Their Way

The next day started out hotter than a sunburn.

Mama shook Jem awake and made sure his burlap sack was ready to go.

She especially made sure Jem's long johns were packed.

Mamas, Jem thought. *They are always fussing.*

He got dressed in a hurry. Long-sleeved shirt, pants held up by suspenders, socks, and high-topped boots.

Jem rubbed his eyes against the rising sun and sat down at the table. A bowl of sticky mush looked up at him.

He made a face and took big, quick bites of his cereal.

It tasted terrible. Like always.

"Don't gobble," Mama said. "Your breakfast will come right back up."

"I can't help it," Jem said between bites. "I'm so excited."

Plop. Ellie dropped a small leather pouch on the table. "You forgot this."

Jem's eyes opened wide. His gold pouch! "Thanks, Ellie."

She sat down beside him. "It's not very full."

"Not yet," Jem said. "But it will be."

He stuffed the pouch in his back pocket.

Ellie gave her brother a big smile. "Fill your pouch with lots and lots of gold nuggets."

Jem nodded. He planned to.

"Fill your pockets, too," Ellie said.

"I will," Jem promised. "I'm going to hit pay dirt. You wait and see."

Ellie's smile grew wider. "If you strike it rich, Pa can buy us a real house. Maybe even a brick house in town."

She let out a wishful sigh. "Like Will and Maybelle's."

Jem choked. His last bite of mush nearly

came up. "Do you have to talk about mean Will and ruin my day?"

He pushed the rest of his mush away.

Ellie ducked her head. "Sorry."

Then she looked up. "Pa's going to deliver Mama's pies while you're gone. He says I can help. It will be fun."

Fun? Pulling the pie wagon to town was *not* fun. It was hard work to keep the wagon from tipping over.

But Jem didn't say those words out loud.

"Let's go, young'un!"

Jem jumped up at Strike's shout. "Bye, Ellie."

He hugged Pa and Mama. "Bye."

"See you in a couple of weeks," Mama said.

"Keep your eyes open, son," Pa said as he ruffled Jem's hair. "You never know when you might trip over a gold nugget."

Jem laughed. Then he whistled. "Come on, Nugget!"

The golden dog leaped up from his spot under a pine tree. They ran together to Strike's side.

The prospector held Canary's lead rope.

Hee-haw! Canary's cry sounded to Jem like, *Let me stay home!*

And no wonder.

The donkey's back was loaded with prospecting tools and supplies. A rope held everything together.

Jem spied his burlap sack. It was tied to the pack. A pick and a shovel hung down from the ropes.

So did a coffeepot and two tin cups.

Strike yanked on his donkey's lead rope. "Let's go." He started walking.

Hee-haw! Canary stomped a foot and then plodded along behind the prospector.

The cups and coffeepot banged against each other. *Clang, clang!*

Jem hurried to catch up.

It wasn't long before they had crossed Cripple Creek, hiked past Bullfrog Pond, and were on their way into the hills.

· ★ ★ ★ ·

The sun was high in the sky when Strike stopped to rest.

At last!

Jem dropped to the ground. His feet were sweaty inside his boots.

His throat felt as dry as the dust under his feet.

And his belly was growling.

"Here." Strike tossed Jem a canteen and a thick strip of jerky meat.

Gulp, gulp, gulp. Warm water poured down Jem's throat.

He wiped his mouth and took a chewy, salty bite of jerky. "How far do we have to walk until we get to the gold?"

Strike looked up at the sun. He looked at the mountains. Then he looked at Jem.

"Young'un, we've barely begun."

Jem ripped off a strip of jerky and tossed it to Nugget. "Have you ever struck it rich?"

With a name like Strike-it-rich, the miner must have hit pay dirt at least once in his life.

Strike laughed. "Would I be livin' in a tent on Cripple Creek if I had me a pile of gold nuggets hidden away?"

Jem took another bite. "I guess not."

He didn't know why Strike lived in a tiny, worn-out tent next to the creek. There sure wasn't much gold there.

Maybe he likes helping Pa and Mama, Jem thought.

He knew the story. So did Ellie.

Long ago, when Pa and Mama first came to the gold fields, Strike had saved their lives.

He helped them stake a claim. He showed them how to pan for gold. He shared his food.

Strike had helped Pa and Mama through their first year.

"Strike's our partner," Pa told Jem and Ellie all the time. "He's closer than kinfolk."

Jem liked that idea. Being Strike's partner was better than being kinfolk.

Partners never paddled your backside, not even when you needed it.

"Young'un!" Strike shook Jem's shoulder.

Jem jumped.

"Time to go," Strike said. "We've got a long hike before dark."

CHAPTER 5

A Tall Tale

All afternoon, Jem walked and walked.

Canary kicked and hee-hawed.

The donkey often stopped and laid his ears back. When he did, Strike yanked on the lead rope and called him a "pesky critter."

Then Canary hee-hawed and kept walking.

It was like a game.

Strike and Canary seemed to enjoy this silly game. They clearly knew the rules.

Jem did *not* know the rules. He stayed far away from Canary's quick kicks.

There was no real path to follow. Strike found animal trails.

"Stick close to me," he told Jem.

Jem didn't ask why. He already *knew* why. He did not want to get lost.

The trail climbed higher and higher all day. It also got narrower.

Right now, the trail was only two feet wide. It twisted and turned next to a drop-off.

Jem peeked over the edge and gasped.

Far below, pine trees looked like pointy spears. The hills were covered with them.

A strong hand grabbed Jem's shoulder. "Careful, young'un. It's a long way down."

It sure was!

Jem had never been this high before. Not even when his family went blueberry picking.

He stepped back and took Strike's hand.

"Looky there." Strike pointed.

Jem shaded his eyes against the after-noon sun. Far away to the west, he saw a flat, hazy valley.

It was miles and miles and *miles* away.

"You can see a lot of California from up here," Strike said. "Ain't it a pretty sight?"

Jem nodded and squeezed Strike's hand tighter. He didn't want to slip over the edge.

When the sun began to set, Strike left the scary trail.

He set up camp next to a clear, bubbling creek. He started a fire.

Jem filled the canteens with icy water. He filled Strike's coffeepot. He found sticks and dead branches for the fire.

"You're a real help," Strike told Jem as he stirred the beans.

Strike fried bacon too. He even gave some to Nugget.

Jem sat down, perfectly happy. This was the best prospecting trip ever!

After supper, Strike leaned back against a big rock. "Have I ever shown you how to dry-wash gold?"

Jem shook his head. "How can you wash gold with no water?"

"It's slow and dirty work," Strike said. "I tried it the year Cripple Creek dried up."

Jem's eyes widened. He had never seen the creek *completely* dry.

"Watch." Strike wrapped his fist around a handful of dirt.

He slowly opened his fist. The dirt poured out a little bit at a time.

Strike gently blew. Some dirt blew away. Some fell into his other hand.

When the dirt was gone, he made his other hand into a fist. He lifted it and poured it out again.

He blew again. Over and over.

His fists went back and forth until all the dirt was gone.

It took a long time.

Finally, Strike opened his hand. Three teensy specks of gold lay in his palm.

Jem sucked in his breath. "It really works!"

"If you're patient enough," Strike said. "Gold is heavier than dust."

Jem knew this. Everybody in the gold fields knew gold was heavier than dust.

Strike brushed his hands together, and the specks fell away. "But I reckon you'd starve to death before you dry-washed enough gold to feed yourself."

He was probably right about that.

"I got bigger plans than blowin' dirt." Strike looked at the mountain creek. "Specially with all this water."

He reached out and ruffled Jem's hair. "I got a feeling we're going to hit pay dirt."

"Me too!" Excitement filled Jem. *We're going to be rich!*

The evening grew darker. And colder. Jem scooted closer to the fire.

His eyelids drooped.

Strike poured himself a tin cup of coffee. "Did I ever tell you about the Spanish fella who hit color near Mariposa?"

Jem's eyes flew open. A gold-rush story!

Pa always said Strike's stories were mostly true.

"Strike has heard many a strange tale, son," Pa told Jem more than once.

"Tell me!" Jem said, wide awake.

Strike sipped his coffee. "It happened years ago. Old Pedro did a fine job of keepin' his diggings a secret. He always waited till dark to go out to his claim."

Jem nodded. *Rule three.* Mind your own business, and don't tell anybody about your spot.

"One day, though, Pedro stopped comin' to town. Folks got worried. They went lookin' for him."

Strike paused. "He had died."

Jem shivered. "Did he fall down a coyote hole?"

"No. The men found a letter in his pocket. It said he got sick and was going to die."

"What else?" Jem knew there was more to this story.

"Pedro's letter said that he'd buried a hundred thousand dollars' worth of gold in his diggings. He was leaving the mine and all his gold to his kinfolk back in Spain."

Jem sighed. So what? "That's it?"

"Nope!" Strike laughed. "The letter didn't say where Pedro's mine was. It didn't give the address for his kinfolk, either."

"What happened?"

"That letter stirred up the miners in Mariposa. They searched high and low. But nobody ever found Pedro's diggings. Or his buried treasure."

"How do you know all this?" Jem asked.

Strike laughed louder. "I was one of the miners who joined the search."

He tossed the rest of his coffee on the fire. It sizzled.

"Now get some sleep, young'un."

CHAPTER 6

Where's the Gold?

Three days passed. Long, hot days.

Three nights passed. Long, cold nights.

Jem wore his long johns under his red-flannel shirt and pants. He wrapped himself up in his bedroll every night.

He was still cold, but he didn't say anything. He didn't want Strike to take him home.

Not yet.

Jem and Strike hiked higher and higher for two more days. They crossed two more creeks.

"Are these different creeks?" Jem asked. "Or is Cripple Creek twisting and turning?"

Strike scratched his beard. "I don't know.

But the snow is still melting. There's plenty of water up here for more than one creek."

Jem slapped at a mosquito. Lots of water meant lots of pesky bloodsuckers.

The mosquitoes pestered Jem morning, noon, and night.

"Where's the gold?" he asked one evening after they set up camp.

Strike stopped short. "Huh?"

"We stop every day and dig up dirt. Then we wash it." Jem made a face. "But we don't find any gold."

Strike chuckled. "That's why it's called prospecting, young'un. Dig here. Dig there. Wash a little gold. Keep looking."

He winked. "You never know when you might hit pay dirt."

Jem looked around. A scary idea pinched his thoughts.

Does Strike even know where we are?

What if they were lost?

"I can find more gold back on my claim," Jem said in a tiny voice.

Strike's face fell. "You wanna go home?"

Jem ducked his head. *Maybe.* Five days was a long time.

Especially when they hadn't found any gold.

Beef jerky didn't taste as good as wild turkey or Mama's rabbit stew.

Jem couldn't drink Strike's coffee. It tasted like creek mud. *Yuck.*

Last night, Strike had burnt the biscuits. Jem gave his biscuit to Nugget when his friend wasn't looking.

But did he want to go home?

Jem's belly said yes. His heart said no.

He shook his head. "Not until we strike it rich."

Strike whooped and slapped his knee. "Now you're talking like my partner."

He pulled a scrap of paper from his pocket. "This here is the reason I keep comin' back to the high country."

He smoothed the paper across his knees. "Come closer."

Jem pressed close to Strike's knees. He looked at the dirty, wrinkly paper. "Is it a map?"

"Not like a map in a pirate story," Strike said. "This paper has just a few marks."

He pointed to a faraway cliff near the

mountains. "See that rocky cliff? It looks like a crown. It's another day away."

Jem looked. The cliff really did look like a crown.

"That's where we're headed." Strike touched two curvy lines on the paper. Then he pointed upstream. "Where two creeks meet."

Jem wrinkled his forehead. *That's it?*

A crown and two wavy lines on a piece of paper?

A sudden memory made Jem sit up straight. "Is that where you went last spring? When you found Nugget?"

Nugget's head popped up at his name. His tail thumped.

Strike nodded. "I try different spots every time I come up here. But I ain't had much luck."

Jem squirmed. He didn't want to hurt Strike's feelings, but his words spilled out anyway.

"Are you sure your map is the real thing?"

"You bet your bootstraps it is!" Strike sipped his coffee and leaned back. "Here's why . . ."

A thrill went through Jem. Another gold story!

"I had a claim by the Merced River ten

years ago," Strike said. "One day, a young miner stumbled into my camp."

"Like Nugget did last spring," Jem said.

Strike nodded. "This fella looked bad off. Worse than your pup. I tended him the best I could."

Jem leaned forward. "What happened to him?"

"He was mighty grateful for my help. He told me about a rich strike up in the mountains. A six-day hike from Goldtown."

Strike took another sip of coffee. "He told me about the crown cliff and the creeks. Then he showed me a nugget the size of my thumb."

Jem's mouth dropped open. "Wow."

"He said there were dozens of nuggets up there," Strike said. "Told me I could have them all."

He let out a long, sad sigh. "Then the poor fella breathed his last."

Jem sighed too. A lot of miners died in the gold fields. It was very sad.

Prospecting was hard, dangerous work.

"I wrote everything down on this here scrap of paper." Strike held it up.

"A real gold map," Jem whispered. Shivers tickled the back of his neck.

Strike put the paper back in his pocket. "I've been lookin' for this fella's claim ever since."

"For ten whole years?" Jem asked, eyes wide.

"Yep," Strike said. "That's how I got my name—Strike-it-rich Sam."

He chuckled. "Only, I ain't struck it rich yet."

That's for sure. But Jem didn't say those rude words out loud.

"Someday, I'm going to find that fella's claim," Strike said.

Jem looked at the faraway crown cliff. It was hidden in shadows. The sun had set.

"Maybe tomorrow," Jem said.

Strike dumped out his coffee. "Maybe. But after that, we're heading home. I don't want to worry your folks."

"Home?" Jem didn't want to think about going home.

Not now. Not after seeing Strike's map.

His belly stopped growling for Mama's good cooking.

He didn't care if the mosquitoes bit him.

Instead, Jem fell asleep thinking about the crown cliff and Strike's map.

Maybe tomorrow ...

CHAPTER 7

Unlikely Discovery

Jem woke up feeling full of adventure.

The sun was just peeking over the mountains. It lit up the crown cliff in orange and pink.

Jem shivered, and not just because he was cold.

That fella's gold strike could be anywhere up there!

Jem untangled himself from his bedroll. He shaded his eyes and thought about where they might dig for gold.

That is, once they got to the crown cliff.

"I need water for my coffeepot," Strike called. He was blowing on a small, smoky fire.

Jem pulled his gaze away from the cliff.

A minute later, he dipped the pot into the icy creek. *Brrr!*

The water was as clear as glass. Jem peered closer.

Could this be the creek with the thumb-sized nuggets?

Jem looked and looked. He saw lots of rocks and sand.

But no gold nuggets.

Nugget splashed into the creek just then. Freezing water hit Jem's face.

"Hey!" he yelled.

The dog lapped water. His golden body blocked the sunlight.

"Scoot over," Jem said. "I'm looking for gold nuggets."

Nugget kept drinking.

Jem grinned. The only gold nugget in this creek was a big, furry dog.

"Where's my water?" Strike hollered.

Oops! Jem jumped up. "I'm coming!"

He ran back to camp. Water spilled over the top of the pot.

"Sorry." Jem set the coffeepot next to a frying pan. Both sat on a wire rack over the fire.

Jem waved the smoke away. "I was looking for those gold nuggets you told me about."

"It won't be that easy, young'un," Strike said, laughing.

Jem slumped. "Too bad."

"I need a hotter fire." Strike pointed to some brush not far away. "Get me some of that drier stuff."

Good idea. Jem didn't want to sit around a smoky fire waiting for breakfast.

He hurried over to a clump of small, dead bushes. They looked just right to make a fire burn hot.

Jem tugged at the smallest bush. It didn't budge.

He grunted and tugged harder, but the bush was stuck tight.

Jem dug his heels into the ground. He wrapped both hands around the thick stem.

Then he yanked with all his might. One . . . two . . . *three!*

The bush came up fast. Jem sat down hard. "Oof!"

He jumped up, brushed off his pants, and lifted his prize.

Dirt and roots hung down.

Holding the clump high, Jem hurried
back to the fire.

"Here you go." He dropped the bush at
Strike's feet. "You can break off the branches
and toss them on the fire."

He grinned. "They'll burn quick, on account of they're mighty dry."

"Thanks, young'un." Strike picked up the bush. "They're just the right size to—"

He stopped. His eyes opened wide. "Well, I'll be!"

Jem's stomach flip-flopped. "What's the matter?"

Strike stared at the clump of dirty roots. "Jem," he said softly. "Take a look."

Jem did what he was told, even though he didn't know why.

It looked like an ordinary dead, dried-up manzanita bush to him.

"Look at the roots, young'un."

Jem studied the roots. They were full of dirt balls, root hairs, and . . .

He sucked in a breath. Was that something sparkly?

It looked like glitter. Gold glitter. His eyes grew as big as Strike's. "Is it . . . gold?"

Strike whooped. "You bet your bootstraps it's gold."

Jem stood frozen in place. He didn't whoop or cheer. He could hardly breathe. *Gold?*

Strike did not sit still. He opened his pocketknife and cut away the root clump.

He found his gold pan and gently laid the roots and dirt in the pan.

"Come on, young'un." He headed for the creek.

Strike's words unfroze Jem. "Wait for me!" he shouted.

Stumbling over rocks and dead logs, Jem ran after his friend. His heart beat like a drum inside his chest.

Jem squatted next to Strike. He was glad his miner friend was swirling the gold pan.

I would drop it for sure, Jem thought. His hands shook.

Strike's hands did not shake. He looked like he knew exactly what he was doing.

Strike washed every speck of dirt from the roots and into the gold pan. Then he threw the bare roots away.

They floated downstream.

Faster than Jem, faster even than Pa, Strike worked his gold pan.

It didn't take long before he had washed the entire pan of dirt away. "Looky here, partner."

Jem peeked into the pan.

Gold dust, gold flakes, and a dozen gold nuggets bigger than corn seeds lay at the bottom of the pan.

Jem gasped. "I don't believe it!"

"It's the real thing," Strike said. "And probably the most gold you've washed at one time in your whole life."

Strike was right about that.

The biggest gold pieces Jem had ever found in Cripple Creek were the size of onion seeds. He needed tweezers to pick them up.

Or Ellie's small fingers.

Strike scratched his beard and chuckled. "It's mighty pretty, ain't it?"

Jem nodded.

Strike patted Jem on the back. "You struck it rich, boy."

CHAPTER 8

Digging for Gold

Jem could not stop staring at the gold in Strike's pan.

Exciting thoughts spun around inside his head.

Pa could buy a real house in Goldtown.

Ellie could have a new dress.

Mama would not have to bake pies to sell. She wouldn't have to wash the miners' clothes.

Best of all, Mama would not have to do the laundry for mean Will Sterling's family.

Yippee!

Jem sat back on his heels. "I struck it rich," he whispered.

"The roots caught that gold like flies in a spider's web," Strike said.

He was smiling as wide as Jem.

When Jem told Strike everything he would do with his newfound gold, his friend lost his smile.

"Hold your horses, young'un," he said. "You struck it rich for a boy your size. But it ain't enough to do all that."

Jem's great ideas went *pop!* He let out a big breath.

Strike laid a hand on Jem's shoulder. "Don't worry. There's probably more gold under that bush you pulled out."

"You think so?"

Strike nodded. "That's the *real* gold strike."

He handed the gold pan to Jem. "This is all yours. Put it away. Then come help me dig."

Whistling, Strike-it-rich Sam went to find a pick and a shovel.

Jem turned back to his gold. He carefully picked out every bit and dropped them into his leather pouch.

Then he closed the pouch tight and stuffed it in his back pocket.

* ★ ★ ★ *

Jem and Strike dug under the bush all
morning long.

Twang, twang! Strike's pick hit big rocks.
He dug them out.

Jem helped shovel loose dirt from the
hole.

By noon, the ground looked like a coyote
hole. Only, it wasn't very deep. Maybe three
feet.

But it was full of gold.

Jem and Strike piled the dirt and small rocks into buckets. Then they lugged the heavy buckets to the creek.

Jem had never washed so much gold! Not in his whole life.

Some gold pieces were small. Other nuggets were as big as Jem's thumb.

Strike dug up a gold chunk as big as his fist.

Jem's eyes nearly popped out of his head. "Wow!"

"This ain't that rich strike up by the crown cliff," Strike said. "But it's pay dirt enough for me."

When they had dug up all the gold in their coyote hole, Strike pulled up a different bush.

They dug and dug. But there was no gold under that bush.

Strike pulled up two other bushes and dug.

No gold under those bushes either.

"I reckon we found all the gold there is around here," Strike said at last.

The old miner looked hot and tired.

Jem was hot and tired too. But he wanted to find more gold.

"Are you sure?" he asked.

Strike nodded. "Prospecting is like that. You find gold. You dig. Sometimes the strike lasts for weeks. Or even years."

"Like the new mine up on Belle Hill," Jem said.

"Yep," Strike agreed. "But sometimes the gold is gone in a day."

"Like now." Jem sat down next to the campfire. It felt good to rest.

The sun was setting. It was too dark to dig any more gold today.

Jem tugged at the two big sacks near his feet. They were both stuffed full. He could not lift them.

Even Strike could barely lift them.

Gold was so heavy!

Jem yawned. "Tomorrow we can look for that other big strike. The one by the crown cliff."

Strike shook his head. "No, partner. We've been gone a week. We're heading back."

"But—"

"No buts," Strike said firmly. "We hit pay dirt. It's time to go home." He looked up.

Jem looked up too. A few stars twinkled in the evening sky.

"I want to be careful not to get us lost," Strike said. "Can't be in a hurry. Not ever. Not in this wilderness."

Jem yawned again. His eyelids drooped.

"It will take a week to work our way down the mountain," Strike went on. "Canary has a big load to carry."

Jem nodded. He had forgotten about that.

Too bad! He eyed the bushes and the coyote hole.

"We only dug under four bushes today. Maybe there's gold under—"

"My mind's made up." Strike dumped his coffee on the fire.

The flames sizzled and went out.

"We can stake a claim and come back another time," he said.

Jem sighed. "If we can find it again."

Strike didn't say anything.

That meant he knew how easy it was to lose a claim way up here.

"We've got plenty of gold," Strike said. "Half of it's yours, partner."

He winked at Jem. "There's plenty for some of those plans you told me about."

Jem cheered right up. "Yes sirree!"

CHAPTER 9

Trail Trouble

Strike and Jem packed up bright and early the next morning.

Jem rolled up the bedding. He tied the coffeepot, the shovels, and the picks to Canary's pack.

He found a spot for the gold pans and stuffed them in.

Strike tied the two sacks of gold together. Panting and puffing, he slung the load across the donkey's shoulders.

A heavy sack hung down on each side.

Hee-haw! Canary laid back his ears and snapped his teeth at Strike.

He did not like this extra load on his back.

Strike paid no attention. "Let's go," he told Jem.

Going downhill was slower than going uphill.

It was scarier, too.

Loose rocks and dead branches made the ground slippery.

Jem held his breath and hung on to Strike's hand.

For three whole days they picked their way through the pine forests and beside rushing creeks.

Nugget ran ahead and bounded back. The steep path did not seem to bother him.

The steep ground bothered Canary, though. Twice he sat down.

Strike worked hard to talk his stubborn donkey into getting up.

Poor Canary! Jem felt sorry for him. He had a heavy load.

Two days later, Jem was very tired. He could hardly keep his eyes open.

He wanted to sleep on his own cot.

He missed Pa and Mama. He even missed Ellie.

I'm tired of walking, he thought. *I'm tired of slipping and sliding.*

Jem especially didn't want to slip right now. He didn't want to fall over the steep edge.

It was a long drop to those pine trees that looked like pointy spears.

Just then, Canary slipped and lost his footing. He kicked out his hooves.

Hee-haw! Hee-haw!

Then everything happened at once.

Strike gave Jem a big push. He fell hard against a pine tree.

His head spun. Black spots danced in front of his eyes. He blinked and sat up.

"Strike!" Jem yelled. "Where are you?"

He could not see his miner friend anywhere. Had he fallen over the edge?

Please God, no! Jem prayed.

He jumped up. He felt dizzy, but he stayed on his feet. "Strike!"

There was no answer.

Hot tears stung Jem's eyes. Where was Strike?

Nugget barked and sniffed at Canary.

Then Jem saw Strike's legs. They poked out from under Canary.

He gasped. "Oh, no!"

The donkey had fallen over. Right on top of Strike.

Canary lay only inches away from the drop-off. He couldn't get up.

He thrashed and kicked, but the heavy gold sacks and the pack held him down.

One hoof kicked a gold sack. It slipped over the edge and hung down.

Strike groaned. He could not get out from under Canary.

Not with the heavy sacks holding the donkey down.

"Jem!"

Jem ran to Strike's side. "What should I do?"

Strike sucked in a breath. He sounded hurt. "Get your knife. Cut the rope. Then Canary can get up."

Jem didn't move. "Cut the rope?"

If he cut the rope, all the gold would drop into the deep valley below.

Canary *hee-hawed* and lay still.

"Do it! Strike said.

Jem jammed his hand in his pocket. He brought out his knife.

Then he crawled on his hands and knees to the very edge of the cliff.

Jem's whole body shook with fear.

Fear that he would fall over the edge.

Fear that Canary might be dragged off the cliff.

Fear that Strike was badly hurt.

And . . . fear that they would lose all the gold he and Strike had found.

"Hurry, partner." Strike's voice had grown weaker. His eyes closed.

Jem peeked over the edge. Both sacks hung down now. The rope was tangled up with the pack.

He looked at the gold. He looked at Canary. Then he looked at Strike.

Strike opened his eyes. "Do it, Jem. If Canary starts thrashing again, he'll go over."

Jem opened his knife. He sawed at the rope. Back and forth. Back and forth.

Snap! The rope broke.

Down, down, down plunged the gold sacks.

Down, down, down plunged Jem's great plans for his family.

He watched until the sacks looked like

two little marbles. Then they fell into the thick forest and were gone.

Canary jerked to his feet. He shook his head and stretched out his neck. *Hee-haw!*

It sounded like he was saying, *Good riddance.*

Jem scooted away from the edge. He blinked back tears. "All the gold is gone."

"Jem."

Jem looked up. If only Strike had not been trapped under Canary!

The miner was strong. He could have lifted the gold sacks away from the donkey.

If only . . .

Jem choked back a sob.

Strike scooted away from the edge and sat up. "Come here, young'un."

Jem fell into his friend's arms.

Strike let Jem cry for a long time.

CHAPTER 10

Home at Last

Jem felt better after his tears dried up. Then he got a big surprise.

Strike was wiping tears from his own eyes.

"Ya know what your pa would say right now, young'un?"

Jem shook his head. He couldn't talk.

His tears were gone, but a big lump was stuck in his throat.

Strike smiled. "He'd tell you it's not right to put your hopes on earthly treasure."

Jem ducked his head. Yep, that's what Pa would say, all right. Mama too.

Pa didn't have what folks called gold fever. He didn't drag his family from gold camp to gold camp, hoping to strike it rich.

Not Pa. He was happy when he found enough gold to take care of his family.

Strike was right. Pa liked to put his hopes on heavenly treasure.

But Jem didn't say anything. His heart still hurt.

"The gold is gone, young'un," Strike said. "It's a shame, but at least we're all right."

He tried to stand, but he fell back down. "Well, *you're* all right. I got me a bum ankle."

Jem's eyebrows shot up. He found his voice. "You're hurt?"

"Canary wasn't gentle when he fell on me." Strike winced. "Go get that pesky critter. I'll have to ride him home."

Jem did not like Canary. Canary didn't like Jem.

But Jem clenched his jaw and went after him.

Nugget helped. He growled at Canary and made him stand still.

Hurrah for Nugget!

An hour later, most of Canary's pack was on the ground. Strike sat on the donkey.

The old miner let out a deep breath. "I

don't feel too good, partner. You'll have to get us home."

Jem's belly flip-flopped. "I . . . I don't know the way."

Strike pointed at Nugget. "Didn't that dog find Ellie when she was lost?"

"Yes."

"Well then?" He waved his arm. "Tell him to go home. Then follow him."

And that's just what Jem did.

· ★ ★ ★ ·

Two days later, Jem crossed Cripple Creek. He yanked on Canary's lead rope. "Come on."

The donkey plodded through the muddy trickle behind Jem. He didn't even twitch.

He was the best-behaved donkey ever.

No wonder. Nugget nipped his legs if he didn't obey.

Strike sat on Canary's back, half asleep. He was slumped over the donkey's neck.

Ellie saw them first.

She waved. Then she shrieked, "Pa! Mama! Jem's back!"

All three came running.

Mama's face turned pale when she saw how dirty Jem was. And how tired.

"Jeremiah," she scolded, "what on earth happened?"

Pa hushed her when he saw Strike. "Ellen, help me with Strike."

When everybody was settled, Jem sat on Pa's lap. He leaned against his chest and yawned.

He was too tired to talk, so Strike told their story.

The miner turned their adventure into an exciting gold tale. Just like they were real gold prospectors.

Which they were.

"Show them your gold, partner," Strike told Jem.

Jem dug out his small gold pouch. It was filled nearly to the top.

Ellie *oohed* and *aahed*. "It's really true!"

Jem laughed. "Of course it's true."

"Maybe a prospector will explore that valley someday," Ellie said. "He might find those two sacks."

Strike winked at Jem. "I might try it myself someday."

Jem didn't say a word. But he was thinking a lot.

If their story turned out like most miners' tales, nobody would ever find that gold.

Not even Strike.

It was probably lost for good.

"At least I finally lived up to my name," Strike was saying. "Strike-it-rich Sam struck it rich. Pounds and pounds of gold."

"You sure did," Jem said.

Strike cocked his head at Jem. "And don't forget, young'un. I still got that map to the crown cliff and those two creeks."

Jem's heart leaped. "That fellow's gold claim is up there somewhere."

"When I go again, do you want to come along?" Strike asked. His eyes twinkled.

Before Mama could say no, Jem yelled, "Yes!"

A Peek into the Past:
Gold Tales

The stories Strike told Jem around the campfire are true. The gold Jem found when he pulled up the manzanita bush is also based on a true story.

Here are two more gold tales.

In one gold town, two men were locked up for a crime. The men didn't like their stay, so they dug a tunnel to escape. As they dug deeper under the jailhouse, the men hit a big pocket of gold.

When their jail term ended, the men did not want to leave. They wanted to dig more gold.

Another story tells about a hunter who came across an old, run-down cabin in the mountains. The roof was caved in. Trees were growing inside the cabin. The hunter found a gold pan full of gold nuggets.

The hunter returned to camp and showed his partner the nuggets. They bought more supplies in town and went back to look for the cabin. They also wanted to find the gold diggings that had produced those nuggets.

The hunters spent many days looking. They went back every spring and summer for years and years to search. But they never found that old cabin. Or the gold diggings.

Even today, the "lost cabin" mine may still be waiting for someone to find it.

· ★ ★ ★ ·

Download free coloring pages and learning activities at GoldtownAdventures.com.